THE MEMORY
of an ELEPHANT

AN UNFORGETTABLE JOURNEY

By Sophie Strady

Illustrations by Jean-François Martin

chronicle books · san francisco

Marcel is an elephant—a very old elephant. Like all elephants, his skin is gray and wrinkled, so it is difficult to tell his exact age.

An elephant sleeps little and usually standing, always on alert. Not more than three or four hours are spent lying down each night. During the day, an elephant takes naps . . . standing up!

"Well, what day is it?" Marcel asks, stretching out in his bed.

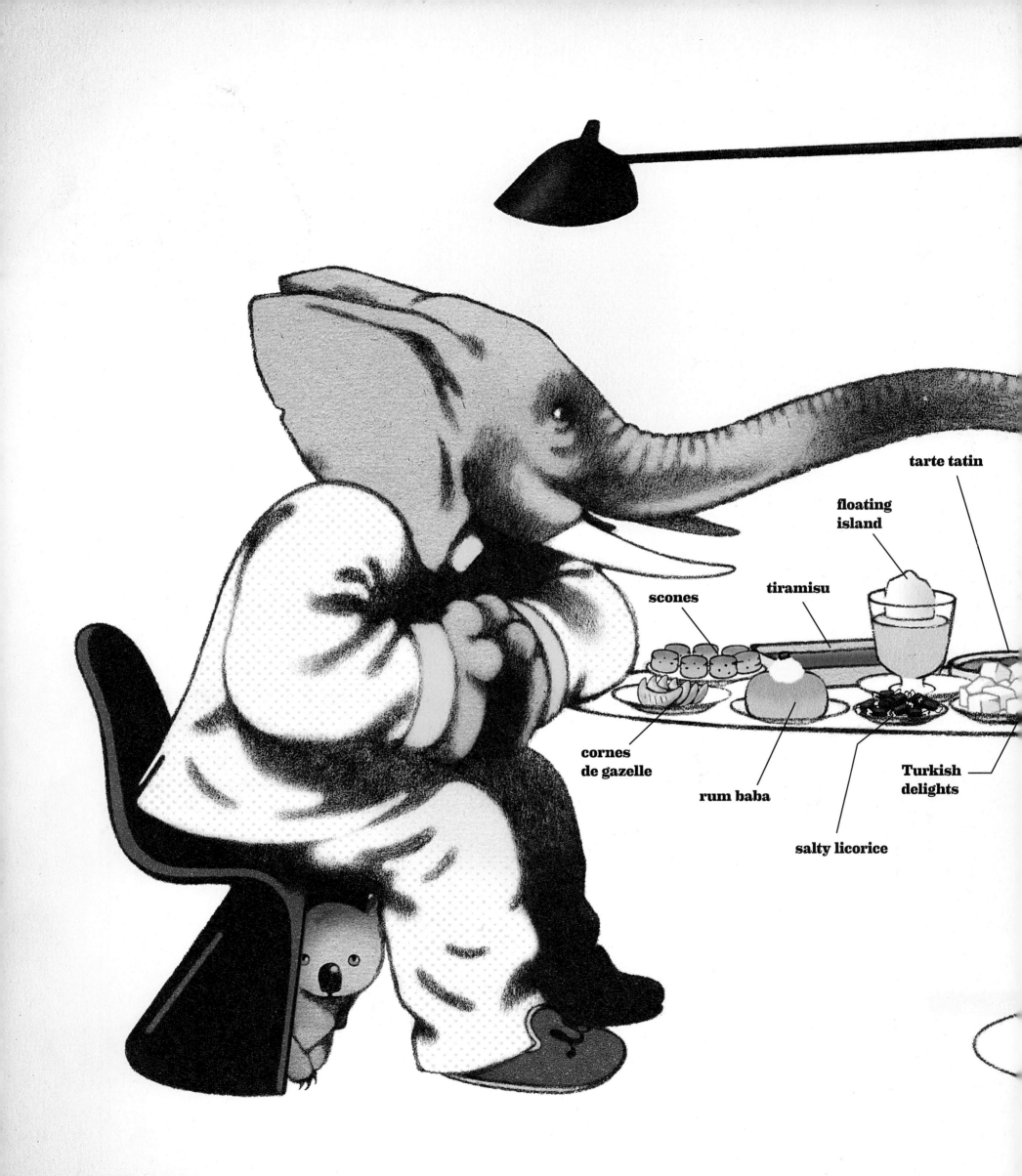

tarte tatin

floating
island

tiramisu

scones

cornes
de gazelle

rum baba

Turkish
delights

salty licorice

Marcel heads downstairs to the kitchen, where he discovers a buffet of gourmet treats from all over the world: heaps of raisin scones, cornes de gazelle, delectably soft Turkish delights, a stack of piping-hot crêpes, an enormous tiramisu, a tarte tatin, fortune cookies, green tea ice cream, a generous bunch of bananas, and even salty licorice.

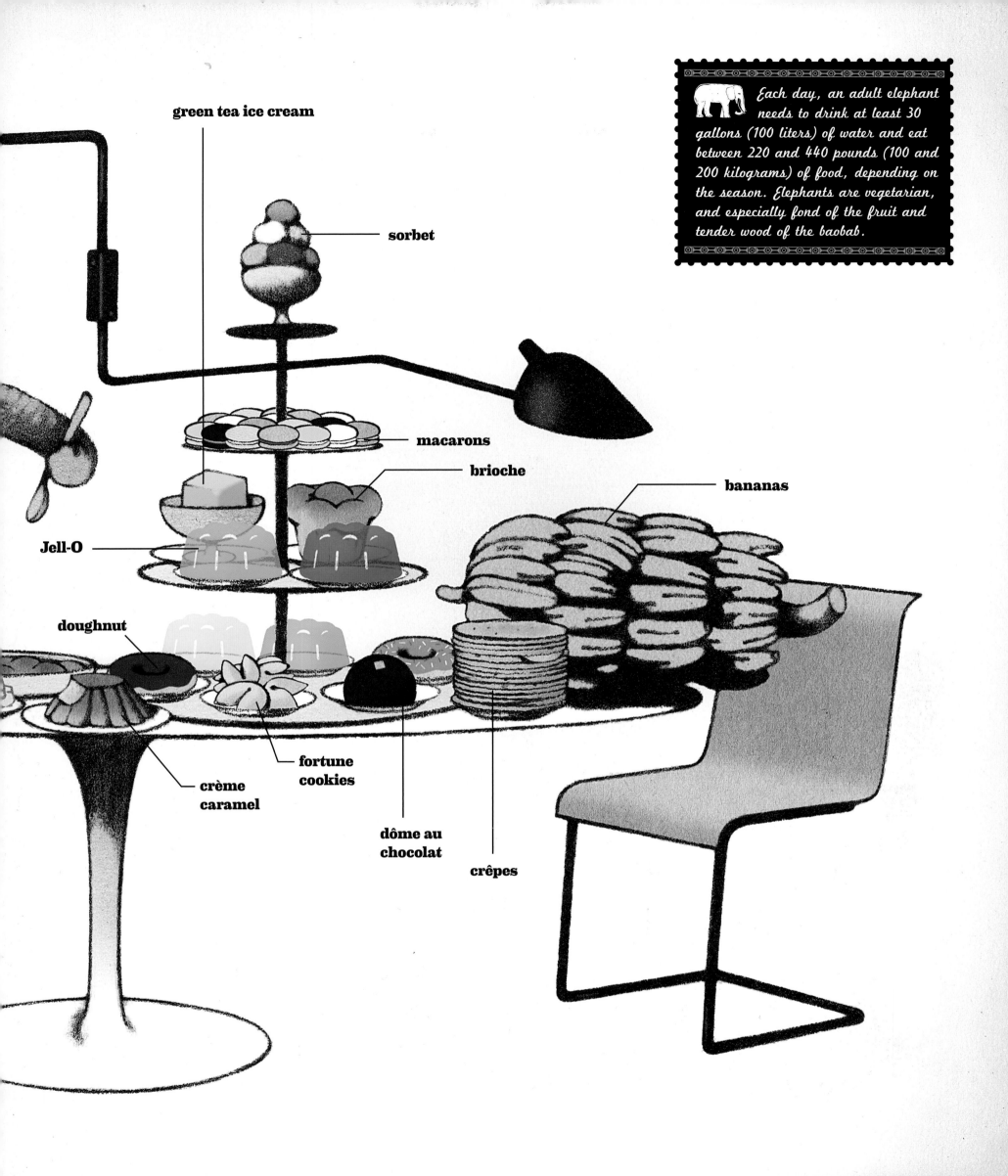

green tea ice cream

sorbet

macarons

brioche

bananas

Jell-O

doughnut

crème caramel

fortune cookies

dôme au chocolat

crêpes

"What delicacies!" Marcel exclaims, sitting down to the feast. "Who has prepared this breakfast of kings?"

The **skin** of an elephant is very thick yet extremely delicate. An elephant frequently bathes or showers with the help of his trunk. He also takes baths in the mud or dust to protect his skin against the sun's rays, parasites, and insects' stings.

The elephant appears to have four **knees**, when, in fact, the "knees" on their front legs function more like wrists.

And elephants can't jump: One foot must always be on the ground. Despite their enormous size, elephants don't make any noise when they walk—their feet set their heavy weight down evenly, absorbing all of the shock.

The elephant walks on the ends of his digits, which rest on enormous pads. The **toes** are enclosed in a protective shell, so the toenails aren't visible.

After savoring nearly every morsel of breakfast, Marcel takes a shower outfitted with a big jet of water. He scrubs his tusks, carefully dries his ears, and spends extra time cleaning his nails.

The **ears** of an elephant help him to fan himself: by flapping them, he can lower his body temperature.

An elephant's **trunk** is the extension of the upper lip and the nose joined into one organ, which allows the elephant to breathe. The trunk also helps with smell, trumpeting, as well as with showering, eating, and carrying and caressing its young or fellow creatures. The tip of the trunk is like a finger with which the elephant can shell a peanut. Made up of at least 150,000 muscles, the trunk itself weighs around 290 pounds (130 kilograms).

The older an elephant gets, the more damaged its **teeth** become: This may be why an elephant can die of hunger if it lives to be 70 or 80 years of age.

From birth, elephants have "baby" tusks. The final **tusks**, which serve as front teeth, appear at two years of age. If an elephant is left-handed, like Paul McCartney, then the left tusk is more worn than the right tusk.

An adult elephant weighs more than 5 tons, which is the weight of about 62 men combined! He only digests 40 to 60 percent of what he eats. With his dung, he spreads the seeds of trees and thus contributes to the reforestation of certain regions, just as his enormous dietary needs destroy others.

"Now, what should I wear?" Marcel wonders, surveying his wardrobe, which is filled to the brim. He tries on a variety of outfits and hats, humming all the while, finally selecting red pants with suspenders, and then slipping on very shiny patent leather shoes.

• • • PANTS • • •

Pants get their name from a character in *commedia dell'arte* who was often seen wearing long trousers. During the French Revolution, women who wanted to wear pants were required to ask for permission from the police!

ELEPHANT-HOOF PANTS

In France, bell-bottoms are known as *pantalon pattes d'éléphant,* or *pattes d'eph'* for short, which means "elephant-hoof pants"! Tight at the top and through the thighs, bell-bottoms flare out widely around the ankles. During the 1970s in California, bell-bottoms became popular among young hippies.

THE VEST

The **vest**, called *le marcel* in French, is the ultimate sleeveless shirt: Practical for moving around, it's a popular choice with dockworkers and farmers.

The elephant is smart! In 2006, Happy, an Indian elephant at the Bronx Zoo, was given an intelligence test. A mark was placed on a mirror that Happy was looking at, and she placed her trunk on the mark, suggesting that she recognized her own image! Other animals that passed this test were a few large primates, orcas, dolphins, and some birds.

YOU SAY . . .

➥ **Hats off!** : *Congratulations!*

➥ **Pulled out of a hat** : *Appeared like magic*

The Miniskirt

The first **miniskirt** debuted in a 1962 collection of the English fashion designer Mary Quant, but she may have been originally inspired by a model she saw through a window . . . in Saint-Tropez!

HATS

*People have been wearing **hats** since antiquity: During that time, people wore **petasos**, round hats with broad, flat brims that were secured to the head with a string. Hats of straw were also popular.*

The **block shaper** is the woodworker who sculpts the blocks that milliners use to create the form of their hats. Block shapers also make blocks for bootmakers.

The **top hat** became a symbol of the upper class during the middle of the 19th century.It also comes in a model that folds and unfolds using mechanical springs, which is called an opera hat.

The **boater** is a straw hat adorned with a ribbon. It was first worn by men (particularly athletes) and then by women.

The **bowler** hat was a symbol of great respectability, and was associated with the big city, especially in England between 1890 and 1920. It was intended primarily for servants and peasants because of its durability.

In fashion since the 19th century, the **cap** is light, practical, and equipped with a visor that blocks the sun. In French slang, it's called a *gapette.*

The **bicorne** hat was first used as headgear for equestrians. Today, members of the French Academy or Polytechnique graduates have the honor of wearing it.

THE MASK

This special type of **mask**, which covers just the eyes and is made of velvet or satin, is mainly worn by women.

JELLYFISH SANDALS

Jellyfish sandals are beach shoes made of plastic, with a texture and transparency that resemble the translucent marine critter for which they are named.

CLOGS

Clogs are shoes of wood that closely mirror the shape of the foot, carved from a single piece of wood. They began to appear toward the very end of the 15th century.

THE BOA

The **boa**, a sort of scarf made of feathers, is worn around the neck and looks a bit like the snake that inspired its name. It was worn by elegant ladies at the beginning of the 20th century, and the famous singer Régine sung about it in "La Grande Zoa."

COATTAILS

Coattails, or the **tailcoat**, are a piece of formal clothing that is short in the front and long in the back, and whose black tails against a white shirt evokes a magpie. Coattails are worn for white-tie functions (the dinner jacket is worn for black-tie events). Today, it is mostly classical musicians who wear coattails.

THE EMPIRE STATE BUILDING

✕ 1931 ✕

1,250 FEET (381 METERS) 102 STORIES

One of the tallest skyscrapers in New York City, its top thirty floors were equipped with a sophisticated nocturnal lighting system in 1976. In honor of Martin Luther King Jr., the building lights up in red, black, and green every third Monday in January. On Valentine's Day, it sparkles in lights of red and pink.

Computer Bugs

Even before the term "computer bug" came into use, the inventor Thomas Edison used the word "bug" to describe a "difficulty" or "fault."

The adult male elephant stands about 11½ feet (3.5 meters) tall from hoof to shoulder. Stacking 237 elephants would match the height of the tallest skyscraper in the world, Dubai's Burj Khalifa, which is 2,716 feet (828 meters) high.

The Flatiron Building

✕ 1902 ✕

285 FEET (87 METERS) 22 STORIES

Designed by the architect Daniel Burnham, this New York City building got its name because of its triangular shape, which resembles an iron. In the Spider-Man movies, the building housed the offices of the *Daily Bugle*, where Peter Parker works. However, only the exterior of the Flatiron made it onscreen.

THE SHANGHAI WORLD FINANCIAL CENTER

✕ 2008 ✕

1,614 FEET (492 METERS) 101 STORIES

This incredible building has a summit that looks like a bottle opener. Here you'll find a 180-foot-long (55-meter-long) footbridge, stretching out over an empty space of several stories: This serves as a panoramic observation deck.

THE FIRST IMAC

In 1998, Apple introduced the **iMac**: Its inventive design, created by Jonathan Ive, was comprised of a brightly colored translucent plastic shell on the back of the computer.

TAIPEI 101

✕ 2004 ✕

1,667 FEET (508 METERS) 101 STORIES

Envisioned by its creators as "a majestic piece of turquoise-blue bamboo," the perimeter of the structure echoes the shape of a pagoda. It boasts the fastest aerodynamic elevators in the world (3,314 feet/1,010 meters per minute), and its lights gleam like the facets of a diamond.

THE TORRE AGBAR

✕ 2005 ✕

465 FEET (142 METERS) 34 STORIES

Conceived by Jean Nouvel, the eroded form of this tower evokes Montserrat, a Catalan mountain, as well as the monuments of the architect Gaudí.

THE EIFFEL TOWER

✕ 1889 ✕

1,062 FEET (324 METERS) 3 STORIES

This observatory, created by Gustave Eiffel for the 1889 World's Fair, demonstrated that an openwork structure made of steel and joined by four columns could reach unrivaled heights and resist gusts of wind. Provoking a wave of protests during its construction, the **Eiffel Tower** was once slated to be dismantled, but ultimately became one of the most visited monuments in the world.

KEY DATES IN INFORMATION TECHNOLOGY

✕ ✕ ✕ ✕ ✕

1946 *The first electronic, general-purpose computer, the ENIAC, took up a 150-square-foot (13-square-meter) room and weighed 30 tons.*

1971 *The first microprocessor was invented.*

1974 *The smart card was invented.*

1977 *The Apple II, the first household computer, was introduced.*

1981 *IBM introduced its PC.*

1984 *The portable Apple Macintosh hit the market.*

2001 *The iPod was introduced, along with iTunes, the online music store.*

THE CHRYSLER BUILDING

✕ 1930 ✕

1,046 FEET (319 METERS). 77 STORIES

Wanting to own the tallest building in the world, Walter Chrysler commissioned the American architect William Van Alen to design this building. It was quickly dethroned by the Empire State Building, but it stands today as a beautiful example of the art deco style. The exterior spires of the 61st floor are adorned with eight eagles that are modeled after Chrysler cars' radiator caps.

It is now time to work. Marcel has recently undertaken the monumental task of listing—in an enormous, illustrated encyclopedia—everything he's learned throughout his long and exceptional life. Each morning, the old elephant enters his library, turns on his computer, and then pauses to marvel at the skyscrapers outside. Today, all of a sudden—*tap, tap, tap*—a faint, insistent knocking on the window interrupts his reverie.

What can it be? It is a bird as small as a large fly, and it darts around so quickly that Marcel can hardly make out the path of its flight. "Is that you, Ziggy?" Marcel murmurs, opening the window ever so slightly. Wings whir beside him, beckoning Marcel to follow. Guided by this whisper of wings, Marcel enters the living room where he discovers a mountain of parcels wrapped in bright and patterned paper—gifts in every imaginable shape and size!

14

"But, it's not Christmas, is it?" Marcel asks, winking in the direction of his tiny friend who flies in excited circles above the gifts.

· CUE THE MUSIC ! ·

THE SITAR

The **sitar** is an instrument of plucked strings, used by courtiers in India during the 18th century. During the 1960s and 1970s, it captivated rock groups like The Beatles ("Norwegian Wood" was the first pop song to use a sitar), The Mamas & The Papas, and also the Rolling Stones.

THE HARMONICA

The **harmonica** produces sounds from the passage of air. These sounds change according to how you inhale and exhale through the open reeds. It's popular with musicians like Bob Dylan and Neil Young.

the balalaika

The **balalaika** is a traditional Russian stringed instrument. It is notable for its triangular case and its three strings. It can be played with a pick or with fingers.

THE UKULELE

The **ukulele** is a plucked stringed instrument originally from Portugal, and then imported to Hawaii. It was first made of wood, but since 1950, the Islander and Flamingo models are plastic.

TEMPO
- **Adagio**: *Slow*
- **Allegro**: *Fast*
- **Andante**: *Moderate*
- **Prestissimo**: *As fast as possible*

Elephants can perceive infrasounds, which are very low tones that humans can't hear. This seems to allow elephants to communicate with each other over remarkably long distances (more than 5 miles / 8 kilometers) via sound waves transmitted through the ground.

bagpipes

The **bagpipe** is a wind instrument from Scotland, and it produces a distinctive sound. It is composed of several wooden pipes and a leather sack and is often covered in sheepskin.

NUMBER OF STRINGS

- ✖ : **Classical Guitar** = *6 strings*
- ✖ : **Twelve-String Guitar** = *6 double strings*
- ✖ : **Ukulele** = *4 strings*
- ✖ : **Russian Balalaika** = *3 strings*
- ✖ : **Pat Metheny's "Pikasso"** = *42 strings!*

THE TUBRI

The **tubri**, an Indian clarinet made from a gourd, is capable of hypnotizing dangerous snakes.

THE ELECTRIC GUITAR

The **electric guitar** first appeared in 1931 (the first was the Rickenbacker Frying Pan), adding an electromagnetic pick-up to the guitar that amplified the guitar's volume and intensity. Among the most famous is the Gibson Les Paul, which is played by David Bowie.

THE GIRAFFE PIANO

The **giraffe piano** is nothing more than a grand piano where the case and the strings are in a vertical position. At the beginning of the 19th century, it was the most widespread upright piano. It is typically decorated in an extravagant and luxurious manner.

THE GLOCKENSPIEL

The **glockenspiel** is a percussion instrument that was originally composed of bells, then of metal slats that give it a sound resembling chimes. You can hear it in Mozart's *The Magic Flute* (1791) as well as in The Beatles' "Being for the Benefit of Mr. Kite!" (1967).

THE SERPENT

The **serpent** is a bass wind instrument. The twists and turns in its pipe allow the musician's fingers to reach the holes that regulate the instrument's sounds.

DECIBELS MEASURE THE VOLUME OF SOUNDS
- *A whisper* = 30 dB
- *City traffic* = 90 dB
- *An elephant trumpeting* = 120 dB
- *An airplane taking off* = 140 dB

THE COMBO ORGAN

This is a small, portable electronic organ, most likely descended from the Italian accordion and made for the stage. During the 1960s, it gave the group The Doors their characteristic sound.

WIND INSTRUMENT RECORDS

Greatest range of sounds:
The clarinet (45 notes)
Most high-pitched sounds:
The piccolo, a very small flute

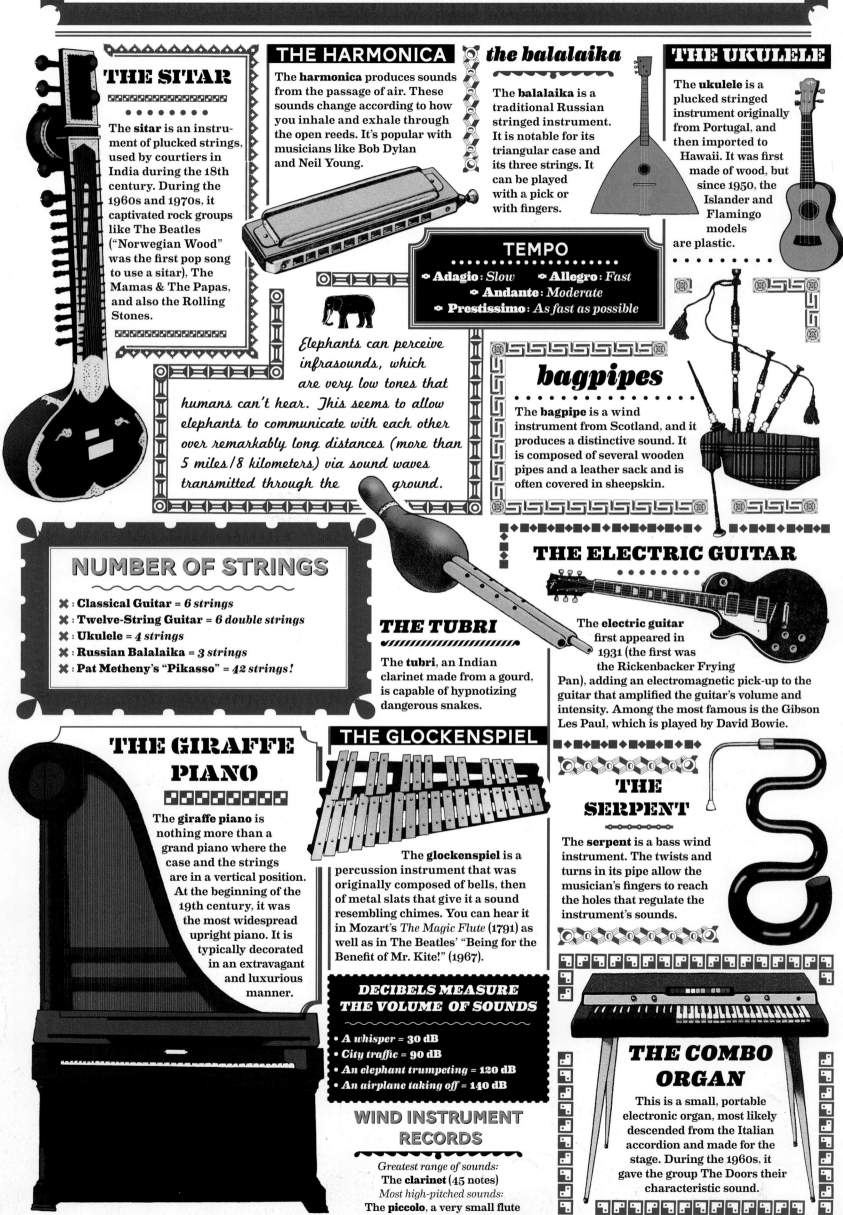

The **helicon**, a wind instrument in the tuba family, is very popular in Eastern Europe, especially in gypsy bands. Boby Lapointe wrote a song of the same name.

Marcel looks closer. On each package, a label displays his name. The largest gift is a strange shape—what could it be? Marcel rips off the wrapping paper to unveil the mystery. It is . . . a tuba—the same tuba he had played in the distant past . . .

✪ In 2013, the world's population was estimated to be around *7,095,217,980*.

✪ Between *6,000* and *7,000* languages (closer to *7,000*) are spoken in the world.

✪ The most-spoken languages in the world: In first place is *Mandarin*. In second place are *English* and *Spanish* (depending on who is doing the ranking). *French* is in 10th or 11th place.

A very long time ago, Marcel formed a band and success came quickly. From all four corners of the globe, fans flocked to the band's wild concerts, and Marcel became a world-famous musician.

One day, exhausted from his endless concert tours, Marcel decided to embark as a simple sailor aboard a cargo ship. The destination: Asia. And so began the elephant's journey around the world. "On those long ocean crossings, I learned how to read a compass, estimate distances, and recognize ships crossing the sea. I became a true mariner!"

· ON THE SEA ·

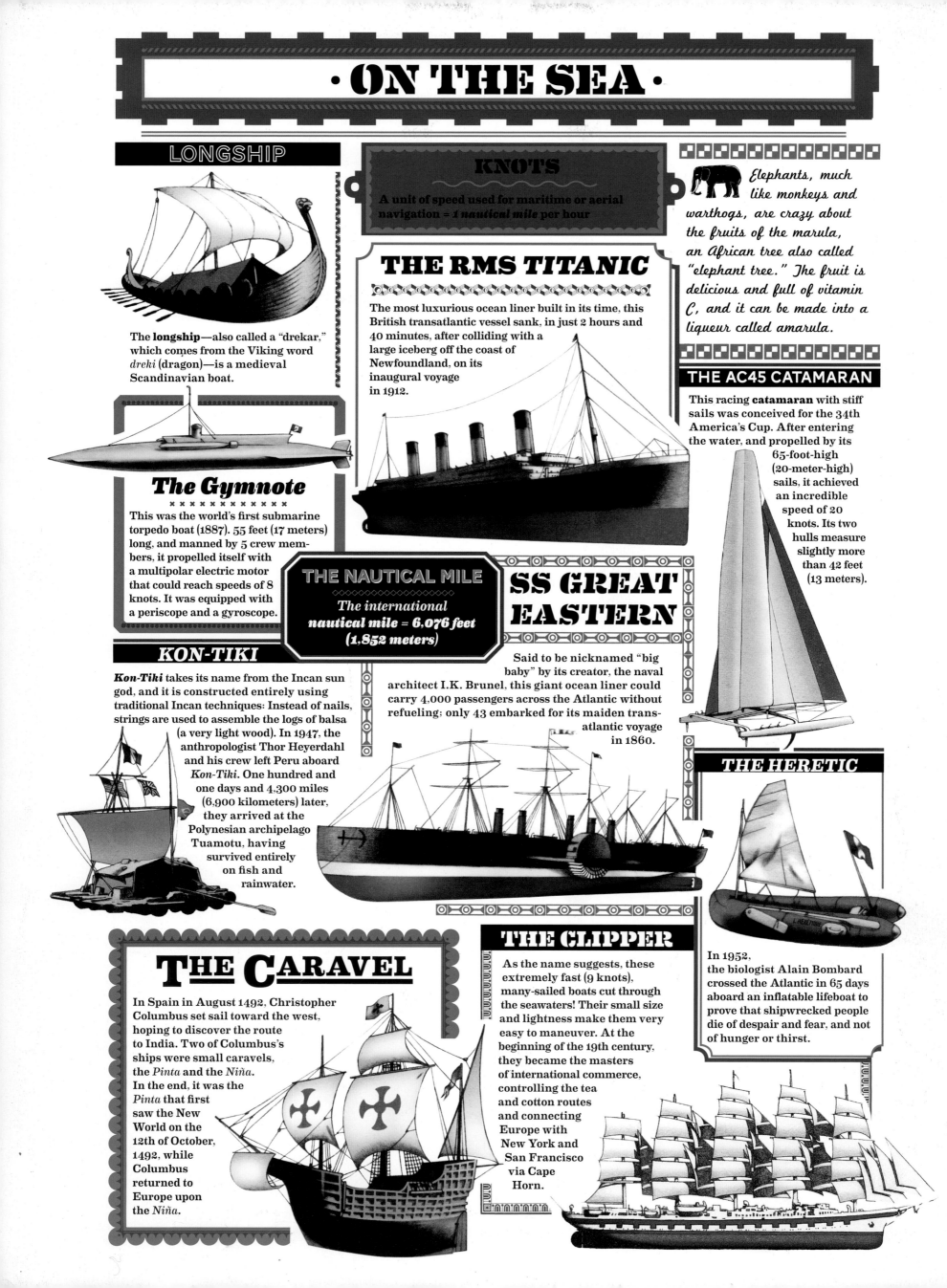

LONGSHIP

The **longship**—also called a "drekar," which comes from the Viking word *dreki* (dragon)—is a medieval Scandinavian boat.

The Gymnote
× × × × × × × × × ×

This was the world's first submarine torpedo boat (1887). 55 feet (17 meters) long, and manned by 5 crew members, it propelled itself with a multipolar electric motor that could reach speeds of 8 knots. It was equipped with a periscope and a gyroscope.

KON-TIKI

Kon-Tiki takes its name from the Incan sun god, and it is constructed entirely using traditional Incan techniques: Instead of nails, strings are used to assemble the logs of balsa (a very light wood). In 1947, the anthropologist Thor Heyerdahl and his crew left Peru aboard *Kon-Tiki*. One hundred and one days and 4,300 miles (6,900 kilometers) later, they arrived at the Polynesian archipelago Tuamotu, having survived entirely on fish and rainwater.

KNOTS

A unit of speed used for maritime or aerial navigation = *1 nautical mile* per hour

THE RMS TITANIC

The most luxurious ocean liner built in its time, this British transatlantic vessel sank, in just 2 hours and 40 minutes, after colliding with a large iceberg off the coast of Newfoundland, on its inaugural voyage in 1912.

THE NAUTICAL MILE
The international nautical mile = *6,076 feet* (*1,852 meters*)

SS GREAT EASTERN

Said to be nicknamed "big baby" by its creator, the naval architect I.K. Brunel, this giant ocean liner could carry 4,000 passengers across the Atlantic without refueling; only 43 embarked for its maiden transatlantic voyage in 1860.

Elephants, much like monkeys and warthogs, are crazy about the fruits of the marula, an African tree also called "elephant tree." The fruit is delicious and full of vitamin C, and it can be made into a liqueur called amarula.

THE AC45 CATAMARAN

This racing **catamaran** with stiff sails was conceived for the 34th America's Cup. After entering the water, and propelled by its 65-foot-high (20-meter-high) sails, it achieved an incredible speed of 20 knots. Its two hulls measure slightly more than 42 feet (13 meters).

THE HERETIC

In 1952, the biologist Alain Bombard crossed the Atlantic in 65 days aboard an inflatable lifeboat to prove that shipwrecked people die of despair and fear, and not of hunger or thirst.

THE CARAVEL

In Spain in August 1492, Christopher Columbus set sail toward the west, hoping to discover the route to India. Two of Columbus's ships were small caravels, the *Pinta* and the *Niña*. In the end, it was the *Pinta* that first saw the New World on the 12th of October, 1492, while Columbus returned to Europe upon the *Niña*.

THE CLIPPER

As the name suggests, these extremely fast (9 knots), many-sailed boats cut through the seawaters! Their small size and lightness make them very easy to maneuver. At the beginning of the 19th century, they became the masters of international commerce, controlling the tea and cotton routes and connecting Europe with New York and San Francisco via Cape Horn.

✪ The **7 continents**: **Asia** (the most people), **Africa**, **Europe**, **North America**, **South America**, **Australia**, **Antarctica** (the fewest people)

✪ The **7 seas**: **Antarctic**, **Arctic**, **North Atlantic**, **South Atlantic**, **Indian Ocean**, **North Pacific**, **South Pacific**

✪ The **8 planets** of the solar system: **Mercury**, **Venus**, **Earth**, **Mars**, **Jupiter**, **Saturn**, **Uranus**, and **Neptune**. The most well-known dwarf planets are Pluto, Eris, and Ceres.

There are between 470,000 and 690,000 elephants in Africa, and around 30,000 elephants in Asia. Nearly 30 percent of elephants in Asia are living in captivity.

The genetic differences between Asian elephants and African elephants are quite possibly too significant for the two varieties to successfully reproduce. A crossbred elephant named Motty, born to a male African elephant and a female Asian elephant, entered the world in 1978, but only lived for about two weeks.

The end of an Asian elephant's trunk has only one lip, while the end of an African elephant's trunk has two. Asian elephants are much smaller than African elephants.

In India, elephants are decorated: Their skin is painted with the colors of the god Ganesha, a deity with the head of an elephant. White elephants are considered sacred animals.

After passing through the Panama Canal and crossing the Pacific Ocean, Marcel reached Ha Long Bay, in Vietnam. His cousin, Ho, a famous geographer, invited him to stay for several months, and so Marcel did just that.

THE SEQUOIA

This conifer is the tallest tree in the world. Some sequoias are 3,000 years old and have reached heights exceeding 328 feet (100 meters). Their trunks are sometimes so big that tunnels are carved right through them. The **sequoia** grows in the United States, and its name comes from Sequoyah, the Native American inventor of the Cherokee alphabet.

Ginkgo Biloba

Ginkgo biloba, known as "the tree of forty crowns," is sacred in China, where it is often planted at temple entrances. It is a dioecious tree, with both male and female forms. It's recognizable by the distinctive shape of its leaf.

THE BAOBAB

The **baobab** is nicknamed "elephant tree" because of its height and its thick bark, or "bottle tree," due to its water-filled trunk. Its bark is edible and also used for weaving and for making ropes. The baobab's flowers, leaves, and fruits, known as monkey bread, nourish humans and animals. In Africa, there is only one species of baobab.

The Firecrest

The **firecrest** is one of the smallest birds in all of Europe and weighs as much as a teaspoon of sugar! The female will incubate seven to twelve eggs and then both parents feed the chicks.

CARNIVOROUS PLANTS

Carnivorous plants live in arid, nitrogen-deficient areas that are poor in mineral salts, so they must find other ways of nourishing themselves. They "eat" many insects, but some also eat lizards, frogs, or even . . . very small mammals.

THE WOODPECKER

Both green and great-spotted **woodpeckers** love trees, whether for rapidly pecking at them (which is also how they mark their territory) or for using the trunk as a place to carve their nest, which they then carpet with wood shavings. This bird makes a snickering sound, just like its cartoon counterpart, Woody Woodpecker (1940).

«FLOWER» SONGS

✗ : *"Hyacinth House,"* **The Doors** (1971)

✗ : *"Orange Blossom Special,"* **Bill Monroe** (1938), remade by **Johnny Cash** (1965)

✗ : *"Petite Fleur,"* **Sidney Bechet** (1952)

✗ : *"Psycho Daisies,"* **The Yardbirds** (1966)

✗ : *"Le Temps des fleurs,"* **Dalida** (1968)

The Asian elephant, more docile than the African elephant, can lift a weight of 661 pounds (300 kilograms) and sometimes assists with moving logs out of forests.

THE LANGUAGE OF FLOWERS

If you want to declare your love, offer **tulips**. **Lilies of the Valley** celebrate youth, while white **roses** stand for purity. A sprig of **holly** signifies happy times!

Edelweiss

Edelweiss lives on mountaintops, at the "nival" level, the area of persistent snowfall where vegetation is rare. White hairs cover its leaves and protect the flower from the cold.

RAFFLESIA

Rafflesia is the biggest flower in the world. It has neither a stem, nor leaves, nor roots, and it can weigh up to 22 pounds (10 kilograms). It has an awful smell, but that's what attracts the flies that fertilize it! There are as many as 15 different types of rafflesia.

TULIPS

The **tulip** is a cousin of the garlic and onion plants. They were first brought to Europe by Austrian Emperor Ferdinand I's ambassador to Constantinople, and later stolen, landing all the way in the Netherlands!

The Owl

The **owl** is a nocturnal bird that can't see very well. During the day, it camouflages itself in its environment and can stretch out and hide its face to look like a tree branch.

THE CACTUS

The **cactus** is capable of modifying its leaves to become thorns (or of not having leaves at all) to reduce its perspiration. Cacti can be enormous or very small, and can come in rather monstrous shapes.

After months and months upon the sea, Marcel ended his voyage in Paris. Since he was such a strong elephant, Marcel was hired to tend the trees in the beautiful Luxembourg Gardens. Every afternoon, when his work was done, Marcel would laze in the sunshine, savoring the flowers' subtle scents, and watching the children sail their toy boats upon the pond.

It is said that mice scare elephants, when, in fact, elephants are scared by . . . bees! In 2007, the research team of animal scientist Lucy King discovered that more than 90 percent of elephants flee when they hear bees humming. In certain regions of Africa, a barrier of beehives provides an effective solution for keeping hungry elephants from eating the food from farmers' land.

It was May 1968.* Suddenly, there was chaos in the streets! Students sent a current of protest across the city of Paris—and even through the Gardens' beehives! Marcel ran out from beneath the trees and was suddenly in the middle of the fray. He found himself chanting with the crowd: "In May, we'll have our way! In May, we'll have our way! In May . . ."

*This was a time of worker strikes and civil unrest in France.

Elephants are particularly social and considerate animals. They touch and pet each other with their trunks, which they also interlace with one another. Elephants worry about weak or injured members of their group and seem to be affected by a death in their herd.

But back to this very moment, far from that tumultuous time. Marcel notices a cardboard tube that has not yet been opened. It is a poster, and it reads: *In May, we'll have our way!*
"We are certainly in May!" he says. Ah, so that's it: The reason for the breakfast! The gifts! Ziggy's unexpected visit! Marcel was born on May 1, May Day. Today is his birthday!

Suddenly, Marcel senses a rustling behind him. Under sofas, curled in drawers, hidden behind chairs and tables, and camouflaged by curtains and cushions, a crowd of animals now emerges, little by little, from their hiding places. Everyone has been waiting for the old elephant to open not only his presents, but the doors of his memory.

And yet, Marcel does not seem surprised by his guests' presence. "What a pleasure to see you here, my dear friends!" With one dramatic sweep of his trunk, Marcel lifts a curtain, revealing the biggest and most beautiful cake anyone has ever seen.

"I thought you might come to wish me a happy birthday. So, to celebrate our friendship, let's go outside and be merry! We'll dance the night away beneath the stars!"
And they do. The animals must squeeze onto the terrace, but no one seems to mind, as the night is electric with music, and fireworks splash across the warm May sky.

RECIPE FOR "LA CRÊPE MARCELETTE"
(with banana!)

☞ *To be made with an adult*

FOR THE BATTER (TO SERVE 10 HUMANS OR 1 ELEPHANT), YOU NEED:

➤ *About 1 cup (125 grams) all-purpose flour*
➤ *2 eggs plus 1 egg yolk*
➤ *2 cups (480 milliliters) whole milk*
➤ *3 tablespoons melted salted butter, plus more for the pans*
➤ *1 vanilla pod*
➤ *Pinch of salt*
➤ *5 bananas, sliced*
➤ *Pinch of brown sugar*
➤ *½ lemon*

1 In a large bowl, make a well with the flour, add the eggs and yolk, and mix with a fork. Slowly incorporate the milk, then the melted butter, vanilla pod, and salt, and mix with a whisk. You can also mix everything, in the same order, with an electric mixer.

2 In a medium pan, brown the sliced banana pieces for a few minutes in a mix of butter and brown sugar.

3 Heat a large pan, and then add a bit of butter, distributing it evenly over the surface. Pour in some batter to create the crêpe. When it turns yellow, takes shape, and bubbles at the edges, flip the crêpe over with a spatula.

4 Delicately place some banana slices on the crêpe and close the crêpe around them, forming a square. Slide the folded crêpe onto a plate and repeat with the remaining batter. Squeeze a bit of lemon over everything. Enjoy!

MARCEL IS A GOURMAND

pages 6 & 7

MACARONS

✪ **Macarons** are small cookies that originated in Europe in the Middle Ages, but which may have existed, in other forms and called by other names, in many other countries around the world. They're made with almond flour, and they come in every imaginable flavor and color—even purple!

RUM BABA

✪ The **rum baba** comes from Poland, where the word *baba* means "grandmother." During the 18th century, when the Polish King Stanislas I discovered that a brioche he'd brought back from a trip had dried up, a pastry chef named Nicolas Stohrer used alcohol to moisten it, then added dried fruit—and the rum baba was born!

BANANAS

✪ It's not just elephants who adore **bananas**: They are one of the most eaten fruits in the world by humans, along with tomatoes, citrus (oranges and lemons), and grapes!

SALTY LICORICE

✪ Salty licorice are made by Lakrids, a candy company in Denmark. (*Lakrids* means "licorice" in Danish.)

BRIOCHE

✪ **Brioche** comes from Normandy, a region in France. The writer Alexandre Dumas declared that *brioche* comes from the word *Brie*, because the dough for the pastry was first kneaded using the cheese!

CORNES DE GAZELLE

✪ **Cornes de gazelle**, North African pastries infused with orange-flower water, are traditionally served with mint tea. They're made with almond paste.

CRÊPES

✪ People have been eating **crêpes** (see Marcel's recipe on the facing page!) since antiquity. In 494, Pope Gelius I established the holiday of Candlemas on the second day of February—on this day, everyone in France eats crêpes!

DÔME AU CHOCOLAT

✪ The **dôme au chocolat** is a frosted chocolate dessert that has a rounded, domelike shape. One of the most famous versions is the one made by the Parisian chocolatier Pierre Hermé.

DOUGHNUTS

✪ It was the Dutch who first cooked **doughnuts**, making them by frying pastries in pork grease, and it was an American sea captain, Hanson Gregory, who, in 1847, deliberately hollowed out a hole in the center!

FORTUNE COOKIES

✪ **Fortune cookies** are served as a dessert in Chinese restaurants, and they contain small messages, predictions, or funny remarks.

JELL-O

✪ This gelatin-based dessert is called "jelly" in Great Britain. The American brand name **Jell-O** has been around since the 19th century.

TURKISH DELIGHTS

✪ **Turkish delights** are Turkish confectioneries that were first introduced in the Ottoman Empire. They're made using sugar and cornstarch, which can be found in breads, certain plants, and grains. Turkish delights are usually garnished with dried fruits, almonds, or pistachios.

SORBET

✪ **Sorbet** is a dessert that contains no cream (unlike ice cream) and is made by freezing fruit syrup and sugar.

FLOATING ISLAND

✪ The **floating island** (also called "eggs in the snow" in France) is a French dessert made from a base of meringue and custard. The meringue looks like a small floating island on a lake of cream.

CRÈME CARAMEL

✪ **Crème caramel** is a mix of sugar, vanilla, egg yolks, and cream. It has a top layer of crunchy caramel.

GREEN TEA ICE CREAM

✪ **Green tea ice cream** is made from matcha, a green tea powder commonly used in Japan.

SCONES

✪ **Scones**, which come from Scotland, are usually eaten at teatime in English-speaking countries. They can be eaten with sugar . . . or with salt.

TARTE TATIN

✪ **Tarte tatin**, a dessert that originated in a restaurant owned by the Tatin sisters, was born of a blunder: The apples in a traditional apple pie were burning on the stovetop, so one of the sisters decided to pour the pastry dough on top of the apples, put the whole pan in the oven, and then served the tart like that!

TIRAMISU

✪ **Tiramisu** comes from Italy. It is a delicious dessert whose name some people believe means "Take me to the heavens!" Others say that the dessert was originally made from cake crumbs and cold coffee, in order to avoid waste.

MARCEL'S FURNITURE

✪ *Here are silhouettes of Marcel's furniture. It's up to you to find them in the rooms of his apartment!* ✪

✪ **BUTTERFLY CHAIR**
1938
JORGE FERRARI HARDOY,
JUAN KURCHAN,
AND ANTONIO BONET

This chair, made of very solid canvas slipped over a frame of steel tubes, resembles the shape of a butterfly.

✪ **ARCO LAMP**
1962
ACHILLE AND PIER GIACOMO CASTIGLIONI

Inspired by streetlights, this lamp hangs from a curved steel rod, which rests on a marble foot, and projects light below it, much like a ceiling fixture.

✪ **CHAIR**
1931
ALVAR AALTO

Curved wood resting on a base of steel tubes are the components of this chair.

✪ **ANT CHAIR**
1952
ARNE JACOBSEN

This stackable chair is extremely light due to its three legs made of fine steel tubes, and its plywood seat.

✪ **PANTON CHAIR**
1967
VERNER PANTON

Molded from a single block of synthetic resin, this stackable chair was designed by the creator of the Mira-X color system.

✪ **NOGUCHI TABLE**
1941–1948
ISAMU NOGUCHI

This table is comprised of a thick glass surface perched atop pieces of solid sculpted wood.

✪ **DSW CHAIR**
1950
CHARLES AND RAY EAMES

A molded plastic shell forms the seat of this chair, which rests on feet made of maple wood.

✪ **BUTTERFLY STOOL**
1956
SORI YANAGI

✪ **TWO-ARM WALL SCONCE**
1954
SERGE MOUILLE

Made of bent metal that evokes a spider, this wall lamp has a black glossy exterior and a matte white interior.

This stool is made of two identical pieces of plywood, molded to look like wings, which are connected with a brass rod.

✪ AKARI LAMP
1951–1987
ISAMU NOGUCHI

A lamp made with paper from mulberry trees, this piece was inspired by the lamps of cormorant fishermen in Japan.

✪ ELEPHANT CHAIR
1945
CHARLES AND RAY EAMES

Kids can climb atop this molded plywood elephant and pretend to be an elephant driver!

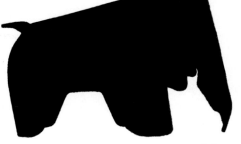

✪ TIZIO LAMP
1972
RICHARD SAPPER

A system of counterweights lets you control where the light from this lamp falls.

✪ TAM TAM STOOL
1968
HENRY MASSONNET

This stool of ultralight molded plastic, originally meant for fisherman, is comfortable and very economical. It's one of the most popular pieces of French furniture in the world.

✪ GRAND CONFORT ARMCHAIR
1928–1929
LE CORBUSIER, CHARLOTTE PERRIAND, AND PIERRE JEANNERET

This comfortable armchair has leather-covered, goose feather–filled cushions sunk into a tubular chrome steel structure.

✪ TULIP TABLE
1955–1957
EERO SAARINEN

This table resembles a sculpture, with its white-grained marble top fixed upon a base of white lacquered cast aluminum.

✪ LC4 CHAISE LONGUE
1928
LE CORBUSIER, CHARLOTTE PERRIAND, AND PIERRE JEANNERET

A chaise longue designed to adapt to the shape of the human body, this chair can be put into many different positions and is covered in leather or cowhide!

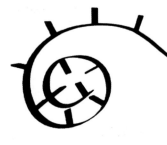

✪ BOOKWORM BOOKSHELF
1993
RON ARAD

A bookshelf made of PVC or colored plastic, the Bookworm takes whatever form you wish, and can be elongated by adding extra segments.

✪ AJ LAMP
1958
ARNE JACOBSEN

With its adjustable asymmetrical head, this lamp lets you decide where to shine the light.

✪ TANK DESK
2008
PETER PETERSEN

Made of lacquered white fiberboard, this desk has rounded angles and camouflaged drawers.

MARCEL'S FRIENDS

★ ***Do you know Marcel's friends?*** ★
They are rare and amazing animals. Unfortunately, they are also often endangered.

❋ ZIGGY HUMMINGBIRD

The **hummingbird**, also called a "bird fly" in French because of its small size, measures between ¾ inch and 8 inches (2 and 21 centimeters), and weighs between ¹⁄₁₀ ounce and ¾ ounces (2 and 20 grams), depending on the species. Some have 1,260 heartbeats per minute, and they flap their wings 80 times per second. Hummingbirds are mostly found in the Americas.

❋ PATTI AYE-AYE

The **aye-aye** is a small lemur that measures around 31 ½ inches (80 centimeters) long. It weighs between 4 ½ and 6 ½ pounds (2 and 3 kilograms), and lives in Madagascar. It is endangered because its habitat is being destroyed.

❋ JIMMY SECRETARY BIRD

The **secretary bird** is a bird of prey that includes several species. It is found in Africa and Madagascar, and measures about 4 feet (1.2 meters) tall and weighs around 9 pounds (4 kilograms). It mostly hunts snakes, but also hunts lizards and other small animals.

❋ PHIL GECKO

The **gecko** is a lizard that lives in warm-weather regions all over the world. Depending on the species, it measures between ¾ inch and 12 inches (2 and 30 centimeters) and weighs between ⅓ ounce and 3 ½ ounces (10 and 100 grams).

❋ JIM FENNEC

The **fennec**, or sand fox, lives in the Sahara desert. It measures between 8 and 16 inches (20 and 40 centimeters) long and weighs just under 4 ½ pounds (2 kilograms). It is an omnivore, eating small animals and also fruit. Like the elephant and the desert rat, the fennec uses its large ears to stay cool.

❋ MOE JERBOA

The long-eared **jerboa**, or desert rat, lives in China and Russia. Its front paws are very small, but it has very large hind paws, which prevent it from sinking into the sand. It also has large ears to help stay cool.

❋ LOU KOMODO

The **Komodo dragon** lives on the island of Komodo, nicknamed "the Island of Dragons." It measures between 6 ½ and 10 feet (2 and 3 meters) and weighs 155 pounds (70 kilograms). This large predator is a protected species.

❋ RYUICHI IBIS

The **crested ibis**, or Japanese crested ibis, is a large bird 30 inches (76 centimeters) long that came very close to extinction. By 1981 in Japan, there were only five left, which were in captivity. Several others were found in China that same year.

❋ MICK MACAQUE

The **Japanese macaque** lives on Japan's islands. Its thick fur allows it to withstand extremely harsh winters. These monkeys warm themselves up in the hot waters of Honshu island's thermal springs. Like other primates, macaques have their own distinct "culture."

❋ TASMANIAN KEITH

The **Tasmanian devil** is an Australian carnivorous marsupial believed to have a very poor disposition. The male can weigh up to 27 pounds (12 kilograms) and measure around 12 inches (30 centimeters) at the withers. It hunts at night, and eats every morsel—including the bones—of the prey it kills.

DAVID CHAMELEON

It is melanin, the pigment present in the **chameleon**'s body, that allows it to change color to camouflage itself. With its eyes, it can see in all directions, and its very long tongue can shoot out at 12 miles (20 kilometers) an hour! It lives mainly in Africa.

ELVIS ORANGUTAN

The two species of **orangutan** live in Indonesia, one on the island of Borneo, the other on Sumatra. These great apes (the only ones in Asia) are very threatened by the destruction of their natural habitat. The male measures around 4 ½ feet (1.4 meters) and weighs between 175 and 200 pounds (80 to 90 kilograms). Researchers have indexed at least 24 elaborate behaviors of orangutans, including the use of tools for fishing.

BRIAN POLAR

The **polar bear** measures between 6 and 8 ½ feet (2 and 2.5 meters). The biggest of them can weigh up to 1,600 pounds (720 kilograms)! Of all the species of bear, it is the biggest, the heaviest, and the strongest. They hunt seals and other animals, and are extremely threatened by global warming and toxic man-made chemicals in the ocean.

RAY PANDA

The **giant panda**, which hides itself in the mountainous forests of central China, eats only bamboo, a plant threatened by farming. It generally measures 4 to 5 feet (1.2 to 1.5 meters) and weighs 165 to 350 pounds (75 to 160 kilograms). As of 2010, there were 1,600 wild pandas in the world.

DAVE PANDA

The **red panda** lives in China in the Himalayas. It adores bamboo, just like the giant panda. It measures about 2 feet (60 centimeters) and weighs between 6 ½ and 13 pounds (3 and 6 kilograms).

RINGO HORNBILL

The **great hornbill** has a large casque that covers its beak. It looks much like a toucan and lives in Asia. It measures between 3 and 5 feet (100 and 150 centimeters) and weighs around 6 ½ pounds (3 kilograms).

PAUL KOALA

The **koala** is an Australian marsupial. In Aboriginal language, koala means "without water": this animal barely drinks anything! It hydrates itself mainly with eucalyptus leaves. It chooses them carefully, as the plant is very difficult to digest. The koala is one of the only animals that eats it.

JOHN LEMUR

The **ring-tailed lemur** belongs to the lemur species and originally came from Madagascar. The destruction of its natural habit has considerably reduced its population. A ring-tailed lemur measures about 15 inches (40 centimeters), weighs 8 pounds (3.5 kilograms), and can jump 33 feet (10 meters)!

YOKO SABLE

The size of the Japanese **sable** ranges from 12 to 18 inches (30 to 45 centimeters), and its weight ranges from 2 to 4 pounds (450 grams to 1.8 kilograms). This animal hides itself well and is very difficult to observe.

GEORGE RHINO

The **rhinoceros** is the second largest land animal, after the elephant. It can measure up to 16 feet (5 meters) long and weigh up to 3 tons. The African rhinoceros, despite its impressive size and its horn, is a herbivore.

JIM LEOPARD

The **leopard** is a large feline measuring 5 feet (1.5 meters) long with a tail of almost 3 feet (1 meter). It lives in Africa and Asia. Very solitary (unlike the lion), the leopard prefers to hide and can even lift its prey up into trees. Certain leopards, black panthers, have fur so dark that their spots aren't visible.

✪ **To my father, an old elephant, who made me love the United States.** ✪
— **The Author**

❋ *First published in the United States of America in 2014 by Chronicle Books LLC.*

❋ *First published in France in 2012 under the title* La mémoire de l'éléphant *by hélium, 18 rue Séguier 75006 Paris, France.*

❋ *Text copyright © 2012 by Sophie Strady.*

❋ *Illustrations copyright © 2012 by Jean-François Martin.*

❋ *English translation copyright © 2014 by Chronicle Books LLC.*

❋ *Library of Congress Cataloging-in-Publication Data available.*

❋ *ISBN 978-1-4521-2903-7*

❋ *Manufactured in China.*

❋ *Design by Katie Fechtmann.*

❋ *Original cover design by Gérard Lo Monaco Les Associés réunis, Paris.*

❋ *English translation by Kate Willsky.*

❋ *Typeset in Eames Century Modern, Marketing Script, and AW Conqueror.*

❋ *10 9 8 7 6 5 4 3 2*

❋ *Chronicle Books LLC*
680 Second Street
San Francisco, California 94107

❋ *Chronicle Books—we see things differently.*
Become part of our community at www.chroniclekids.com.